Lily the Llama Helps Her Herd

by Emma Rashes

Illustrated by Theresa Jahn

*This book is dedicated to everyone who is working
to help their herd during the COVID-19 pandemic.*

Mama flicked on the lights. "Lily wake up!"
It was the morning of Lily's yearly checkup.

Lily got ready to visit her friendly **pediatrician**.

Dr. Leslie helps Lily stay healthy, like a medical magician!

At the appointment, Dr. Leslie said, "you are due for a shot."

Lily thought to herself – *oh no, she better not*.

She worried about the pain and let out a cry.

"It will only be a little pinch," Dr. Leslie replied.

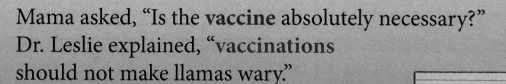

Mama asked, "Is the **vaccine** absolutely necessary?"
Dr. Leslie explained, "**vaccinations**
should not make llamas wary."

"A **vaccine** for Lily
will help our herd stay
healthy and strong.

Brave llamas like her
have helped the herd
all along."

"How do I help the whole herd stay healthy?" Lily asked.

Dr. Leslie responded, "**herd immunity** makes the impact of each **vaccine** vast."

"How does **herd immunity** work?" Lily inquired.

"To help eliminate diseases, **herd immunity** is required."

"Some llamas may be too sick or too young to get this shot.
Your **vaccine** protects the whole herd and helps these llamas a lot."

"This **vaccine** will give you **immunity** from a disease.

Immunity means you cannot get sick so you can be at ease."

"A disease spreading through a herd takes a combined effort to be stopped. It is only when enough llamas are **immune** that the spread will be blocked."

A Healthy Herd Begins with Your Vaccine!

BEFORE → AFTER

"If you get this **vaccine** you can help stop the spread.

The whole herd will feel grateful so there's nothing to dread!"

A Healthy Herd Begins with Your Vacci[ne]

BEFORE → AFTER

"Getting this **vaccine** doesn't only help you,
But your grandma, your neighbor, and baby brother too.

While attaining **herd immunity** is no small chore, your bravery today will protect all the llamas you adore."

"Simply put, **herd immunity** means enough llamas are immune and have gotten **vaccines**.

With **herd immunity** we can help stop infection, And move our whole herd in a better direction."

Dr. Leslie told Lily, "it's only a pinch."

"Okay," Lily said, "I'll try not to flinch."

Lily closed her eyes as Dr. Leslie counted down from three.

"Wow, that wasn't so bad!" Lily shouted with glee.

"Thank you for helping us achieve **herd immunity**, Lily."

"It was really no big deal, please don't be silly."

Dr. Leslie exclaimed, "We are one step closer to **herd immunity**!"

Lily replied, "I'm so happy to help our whole llama community!"

At home, Lily told Papa what she learned word for word.

"Getting a **vaccine** will help our whole herd!"

Glossary

Pediatrician – A pediatrician is a doctor who cares for babies and children.

Immunity – Immunity is the body's ability to stop a particular disease, usually achieved from vaccination or previous infection.

Vaccine – A vaccine is a substance that protects people and animals from getting sick from a particular disease. A vaccine exposes your body to a germ that has been changed so it is safe and will not make you sick from the disease. In the future, your body will remember this germ and prevent you from getting sick from the germ.

Vaccination – Vaccination is the act of using a vaccine to give your body immunity from a disease.

Herd immunity – Herd immunity is when enough people in a community are protected from a disease so the spread of the disease becomes less likely in that community. Everyone in the community is then protected from the disease – not only those who are immune.

Extra vocabulary
Herd, wary, vast, inquire, dread, attain, adore, flinch, achieve

Discussion Questions

- Have you ever gotten a vaccine? What was it like?

- How do you think Lily felt at the doctor's office? Have you ever felt that way?

- How did Lily help the other llamas in her herd? Can you describe a time when you helped your community?

- Do you remember what Lily taught Papa about vaccines? What will you share with your family and friends after reading this book?

About the Author

Emma Rashes

Emma Rashes is a senior and master's student at Stanford University where she is studying biology. She has always loved science and hopes to pursue a career in medicine. Emma wrote *Lily the Llama Helps Her Herd* to share her love of science and teach others about the importance of vaccination!

About the Illustrator

Theresa Jahn

Theresa Jahn has been working as a Graphic Designer for more than 25 years, but has had a love of art since she was a child. Just as she was influenced by creators of educational books, television, and movies, she hopes that her art will be able to tell a story and message to young people that they will remember for years to come.

Acknowledgments

Thank you to my family, friends, and mentors for your support, advice, and edits throughout this process.

A special thank you to Dr. Susan McConnell, Andrew Todhunter, and Dr. Rishi Mediratta for your unwavering encouragement and guidance.

Profound gratitude to Theresa Jahn for your thoughtfulness, patience, and vision and for beautifully bringing Lily and her herd to life.

Thank you to my peers in The Biology Senior Reflection course and the teaching team in the COVID-19 Elective at Stanford University for your invaluable feedback.

Sincere thanks to Dr. Benjamin Lindquist and Dr. Shane Crotty for sharing your input and expertise since the early stages of this project.

Thank you to Dr. Charles Prober, Aarti Porwal, and The Stanford Center for Health Education for making the book more accessible and bringing *Lily the Llama Helps Her Herd* to a wider audience.

Heartfelt appreciation to Dave Rosenberg, the students and faculty at The Rashi School, and the Erickson family for your help in workshopping my early drafts.

Thank you to Dr. Renee Scott for your advice and for providing a space during my Stanford experience to learn about early education and literacy.

Most of all, thank you to my mom for your unconditional support and being Lily the Llama's biggest fan!

Made in the USA
Middletown, DE
02 July 2022